Attack of the Sleep Demon

Taylor Sapp

Alphabet Publishing

Contents

Before You Read

1. How often do you feel tired during the day?

2. How often do you nap? Where/when do you nap?

3. In many countries it is rude to sleep in class but in some countries, it is not unusual. What is it like in your country?

4. Where else is it acceptable or usual to nap in your country?

Attack of the Sleep Demon

It was Taro's first day in his new English class in America. Even though he was excited, he was also a bit sleepy. The large classroom had 12 students from many countries. About half the students (including Taro) were new. They all looked exhausted from their long journeys.

The teacher (who asked to be called Sam and not Mr. Lewis or Teacher) was introducing himself. Then he asked all of the students to stand up! Taro had never done anything like that in his school back home in Japan, so he was shocked!

Sam asked everyone to say two things they liked. He introduced himself first. "Sam Lewis. I love collecting old watches and reading Shakespeare."

Next, a beautiful brown-haired girl from Brazil spoke. "I'm Emily. I like swimming and watching scary movies, but I don't like olives."

Swimming and watching scary movies were Taro's two most favorite things too! He even hated olives! He couldn't believe it! Who was she? His first day and he'd already met the girl of his dreams!

They kept going around. When Taro introduced himself, he said, "I like swimming and scary movies, but I hate the smell of swimming pools." He looked at Emily, who smiled at first, but then a strange sad look crept across her face when he mentioned the smell.

Next to him, a friendly student named Ahmed (who liked "soccer and math but not spicy food") shook his hand with a wide smile. But watching Taro's drooping eyelids, his face quickly took on a serious expression.

"Whatever you do, don't sleep," Ahmed said.

"Yes, I know. The teacher wants us to participate." American teachers really loved this word, the first lesson he learned!

"No. If you fall asleep in the classroom in America, there is a Sleep Demon that will come for you!"

"Sleep demon? That's crazy."

"Do you see that girl over there?"

"Emily?"

Ahmed smiled. "Right. The demon took her ability to smell."

"That's horrible."

"And that boy over there, Teddy. Do you notice anything?"

Sam made all students put their phones on the table, face down. That way they couldn't hide them inside their book or look at them in their laps. Except for Teddy. There was no phone in front of him. Only his textbook.

"The Sleep Demon took Teddy's ability to use a touchscreen. Now he has to use a flip-phone! He keeps it in his pocket because he's too embarrassed, I think!"

Taro couldn't imagine losing the smartphone on the desk in front of him. It was more than a friend to him. A fate like Teddy's would be worse than death!

As the class continued, Taro tried to do his best to stay awake. Sam had lots of energy and was making students talk to each other, which definitely helped. But Taro was so tired! The long flight to the US had been just 2 days ago. Last night he'd played video games most of the night instead of sleeping. Back home, he'd used his two-hour commute to school on the to get extra sleep.

He felt himself nodding off, and though he fought it, Taro was soon asleep. At first, he thought he was still awake, because he was in the classroom and the students around him appeared normal. But instead of Sam, there was someone (or something) very different at the front of the classroom...

It was a monster wearing a dark blue robe. It looked like a demon with two long horns coming out of its head. Its eyes glowed red and two sharp fangs came out of its mouth. It had a long snake-like tail and sharp claws!

Taro heard a loud deep voice in his head, calling him by his full name!

"Ryotaro Hayasabura, you have passed the limit of acceptable classroom sleep. I will deliver an appropriate punishment!"

Red beams of light came out of the demon's eyes and hit Taro. He screamed and woke up back in school. It didn't seem like anything had changed.

***

That evening he discovered the consequences. His parents called, most likely to ask about his day. But he couldn't understand a word they said! He realized everything in his brain that was not English had been erased! He could no longer understand or speak Japanese!

The next morning, to his surprise, Emily sat next to him. She smiled and stared at his extra-large cup of coffee.

"You can't smell it?" he asked. Coffee was one of his favorite smells.

She frowned and eyed him for a moment. "What did it take from you?"

"Everything." He sighed. "I can only understand English now."

"You're not the only one."

"Is there any way to undo this?"

"Yes. You have to sleep 8 hours, every night, in your bed for the next 30 days."

Taro laughed. "Are you kidding?"

"Nope. This is not a joke. It's been 3 weeks now for me. I sleep 8, 9 hours every day. Next week, I will smell again!"

Taro couldn't believe it. 8 hours? At night? He couldn't remember ever sleeping so long in his life!

"But what if I can't?"

She pointed at Teddy. "Six months...His smartphone has been at home, ready to be used aga in...But he plays video games too much..."

As the class started, Ahmed gave him a wink. It suddenly occurred to Taro he'd had never had an English conversation with a girl before!

Was the demon really so evil after all?

***

The next month went by quickly. Emily was able to get her smell back the next week. The two of them spent lots of time together. Sleeping 8 hours a night made Taro feel happier and more energetic than he'd ever been before.

Soon it had been 29 days. The time had gone by quickly! He'd made so many friends, including his new girlfriend! And he'd never even worried about speaking his native language (except with his parents). He almost didn't care when the final night came and he met the demon again in his dreams.

"Ryotaro Hayasabura, you have managed to stay awake in the classroom and get a decent amount of rest. My anger has subsided, and I will return the knowledge that I took from you as punishment!" The demon slowly faded away.

Taro woke up and grabbed a Japanese *One Piece* manga comic book from the shelf next to his bed. He could read it! He cheerfully took the chance to have a long overdue conversation with his parents.

The next day at school, there was a very sleepy-looking new student sitting next to him.

"Hey, you shouldn't sleep," he told the new student.

"But I was up all night. What's the worst that could happen?"

Taro smiled and shook his head. "Well..."

Glossary

claws: the sharp finger and toe nails of an animal

commute : time spent every day travelling between home and work or school

crept: (*here*) appeared slowly

demon: a mythical being that is often scary and harms people

drooping: hanging down

eyed: looked at something carefully

fangs: long sharp teeth, like on vampires or some animals

flip-phone: a phone that opens and closes by folding the middle

frowned: moved the corners of the mouth down, often to show unhappiness

glowed: was bright with light

kidding: lying or exaggerating in order to fool a person

manga: a popular style of Japanese comic books

overdue: should have happened before now

robe: a long piece of clothing that covers most of your body, often worn at ceremonies

subsided: became less or weaker

wink: close one eye and open it quickly, usually to signal to another person.

After You Read

1. Where is the book set? Why is Taro there?

2. What mistake does Taro make?

3. What punishment does he receive?

4. What problems does Taro face?

5. What good things happen to Taro?

6. How does Taro get set free?

7. How would you feel if you got the same punishment as Taro?

8. Do you think the Sleep Demon is good or bad or neutral?

9. What other classroom "crimes" could there be a demon for?

10. Does this story have a moral? If so, what is it?

Writing

Write what will happen next. Do you think the new student will sleep? If so, how will the demon punish them? What will happen to Taro

More Readers

AlphabetPublish.com/Book-Category/
Graded-Reader